0500000676596 5

P9-AOE-992

J Kru
Krulik, Nancy E.
The case of the green
guinea pig
vol. 3

JAN 1 2 2015

The Case of the
Green Guinea Pig

The Case of the
Green Guinea Pig

BY NANCY KRULIK
ILLUSTRATED BY GARY LaCOSTE

SCHOLASTIC INC.

New York   Toronto   London   Auckland
Sydney   Mexico City   New Delhi   Hong Kong

For the ever-mysterious Danny B.

ISBN 978-0-545-26656-7

12 11 10 9 8 7 6 5 4 3 2   11 12 13 14 15 16/0

Printed in the U.S.A.
First printing, October 2011   40
Book design by Yaffa Jaskoll

Chapter 1

Tick. Tick. Tick.

I knew I shouldn't be looking at the clock that hung on the classroom wall. My teacher, Mrs. Sloane, really hates when her students watch the clock.

But I couldn't help it. It was three minutes to three. In just one hundred and eighty seconds, I would be free!

"Jack, I'm over here, not hanging above the door. Please pay attention."

Darn. Mrs. Sloane had caught me.

"Now, don't forget to return your permission slips by Wednesday," my teacher reminded us. "Otherwise you won't be able to go on the upper-school apple-picking trip this Friday afternoon."

Now *that* was worth paying attention to. The upper-school apple-picking trip was a special field trip just

1

for the third, fourth, and fifth graders. This was the first year my friends and I were old enough to go. I couldn't wait.

Rrrriiinnnngggg! Woohoo! There it was: the final bell! School was out for the day. I shoved my permission slip in my backpack and hurried for the door.

"Jack, you want to sleep over after the field trip?" my best friend, Leo, asked me.

"Definitely," I answered. "Maybe your mom will make chocolate-chip pancakes again." I love Leo's mom's chocolate-chip pancakes. My mom doesn't think chocolate is a breakfast food.

There was only one kid in our class who didn't seem excited to go apple picking. Charlie looked miserable as we all filed out into the hallway. His eyes were watery, and he kept wiping his drippy nose with this crinkled, wet tissue he kept in his pocket.

"I hate being around trees," Charlie said. "They make me sneeze."

"Everything makes you sneeze, Snotman," Trevor the Terrible said. He's the meanest kid in the third grade.

Charlie's watery eyes got even more watery. I could tell he hated Trevor's nickname for him. Who wouldn't?

"Aachoo!" Charlie sneezed.

"See?" Trevor said. "More snot."

"You make plenty of snot, too," Elizabeth Morrison told Trevor.

Trevor shoved his nose at her. "No way! You see any boogers hanging out here?"

"Everybody makes boogers," Elizabeth told him. "The average human nose makes about a quart of snot every day."

"How do you know that?" Trevor asked her.

"I read it in a science book," Elizabeth explained.

"Who reads science books for fun?" Trevor wondered out loud.

Elizabeth, that's who, I thought. She's the school Brainiac, after all. I was really impressed that Elizabeth was brave enough to stand up to Trevor. He was the biggest, meanest kid in the third grade. You got the feeling he could squash you like a bug if he wanted to.

But Elizabeth just stood there staring back at him. I could tell she was a little nervous, though, by the way she was playing with one of the red, wormy curls that dangled around her head.

I know a lot about Elizabeth. She's my partner in our detective business. We solve mysteries together. Elizabeth is a good partner to have because she's supersmart, and she's brave enough to stand up to anyone — even Trevor the Terrible.

Trevor was about to say something to Elizabeth, but he was stopped by a fifth grader wearing a bright-orange school safety sash across her chest.

"Keep it moving," she said.

"You're so bossy, Maxine," Trevor said.

I rolled my eyes. Trevor was pretty bossy himself.

"It's my job to keep the halls safe," Maxine told Trevor. "That's what fifth-grade school safeties do." She turned suddenly as she spotted three fourth graders running past her. "No running in the halls!" Maxine called after them.

But they ignored her — all except the one kid who turned around and stuck his tongue out.

"I'm going to report you," Maxine shouted. *"You can't just ignore a safety!"*

Actually, they could. In fact, that's exactly what they were doing.

"What are you staring at?" Maxine snapped at Trevor, Leo, Elizabeth, and me. "Don't you have a bus to catch?"

She didn't have to ask twice. Maxine was obviously in the mood to report somebody for something. And I sure didn't want that somebody to be me.

My five-year-old sister, Mia, was sitting on the lawn outside my house when I got off the bus. Mia's in half-day kindergarten, so she gets home way before I do.

"You want to play house?" Mia asked as I walked up the driveway.

Oh yeah. Like *that* was ever going to happen.

6

I thought about ignoring her, the way those fourth graders had ignored Maxine. But Mia would just tell my mom I was being mean. That was her way of "reporting," which is pretty much the same as tattling. So I said, "Not today. I've got stuff to do."

Suddenly, I heard a voice yell out, "Hey, Big Head! Look out below!"

I looked up to see two squirrels — one with buck teeth, and the other with a bite taken out of his ear — sitting on a branch in the oak tree. The squirrel with the bite mark threw an acorn right toward me.

His aim was pretty lousy. Instead of heading for me, the acorn was making a beeline straight for Mia.

"Watch out!" I shouted. I pushed her out of the way.

Bam! Mia landed right on her rear end. "Hey! What was that for?" she shouted.

Plop. The acorn landed on the ground about two inches from Mia's head.

Mia scrambled to her feet and started running to the house. "Mommy!" she shouted. "Jack pushed me for no reason!"

That was not true. I *did* have a reason to push Mia out of the way of that incoming acorn. A really good reason.

Chapter 2

It all started one day when I was taking my dog, Scout, out for a walk in the yard. Those same two squirrels were doing some target practice with acorns. Unfortunately, the target they were aiming for was my head. And unlike today, Zippy — that's the one with the bite taken out of his ear — got me good.

Ordinarily, the only thing an acorn bash to the head would have left me with would have been a lump. But the oak tree in my front yard is a magic tree. *Seriously.* If a human gets hit with an acorn from that tree, he gets special powers — like being able to talk to animals.

A magic tree? I didn't believe it at first, either. But Zippy and Zappy, the two squirrels who live in the tree, told me. And once I realized I could understand two squirrels, I figured there was something to their story

9

about the magic tree. Ever since that day, I've been able to talk to Zippy, Zappy, my dog Scout, and all the other animals in the neighborhood.

That was why I had pushed Mia out of the way. I didn't know what kind of special ability she might wind up with if she got bonked on the head with an acorn. All I knew was the last thing I needed was for Mia the Pain to get her own superpower.

"You're home! You're home!"

I didn't have time to wonder about what my mom was going to say about me pushing Mia, because at just that second, Scout came bounding out of the house.

"Wanna play fetch?" he barked at me. "Get a ball! Get a ball!"

"In a minute," I said. "First I've gotta go inside and give Mom this permission slip before I forget."

"Permission?" Scout asked. "Permission for what?

"To go apple picking," I told him.

"Ohhhh! Apple picking," Scout said. "I wanna go apple picking. I've *always* wanted to go apple picking." He stopped for a minute. "What's apple picking?"

I laughed. "You're such a dope," I teased, scratching his chin.

"You can say that again," a soft voice purred behind me. I turned around to see Shadow, the gray cat from next door, slinking toward us. "Dogs are *very* dopey."

"Oh yeah?" Scout said. His ears flattened against his head and his tail dropped. "If you're so smart, why don't *you* tell us what apple picking is?"

Shadow gently licked one of her paws. "Simple. Apple picking is something humans do that I have absolutely no interest in."

"That's a dopey answer," Scout said. "*You* must be the dope around here."

Shadow arched her spine and puffed up the fur on her back. I could tell she was ready for a fight. "You'll be sorry you said that, drool for brains," she hissed.

"Hey, Scout, y'all wanna play?" Just then a beagle puppy with a black heart-shaped spot on her back came bounding over. Her long white tail was wagging happily behind her.

"Josie's here!" Scout cheered. His tail started to wag, too.

"Hey there, Scout," Josie said in her soft Southern drawl.

Josie is our neighbor's new puppy. She's from a rescue group in Arkansas, so she sounds a little different than the other dogs, at least to me. I'm pretty sure most people don't realize her bark has a Southern accent.

"Oh great," Shadow sneered. "Just what we need around here — another bone-eating bonehead."

"Watch it, mouse breath!" Josie growled at her.

"Who are you calling mouse breath?" Shadow hissed back.

"Well, if the fur ball fits —" Josie began.

Shadow hissed again and showed her claws.

"Oh my," Josie drawled. "You have kitty litter under your nails!"

"At least I use a litter box," Shadow told her. "You pee on the sidewalk. Now *that's* gross."

"Y'all are gonna be sorry you said that," Josie growled.

Uh-oh. Josie's tail had just dropped. She wasn't kidding about making Shadow sorry for what she'd said.

"Shadow, maybe you should go," I told her.

Shadow sighed and licked her paw slowly. "I'm not worried. Her bark is worse than her bite."

"Wanna bet?" Josie barked.

Shadow hissed and then leaped up and landed on a low branch of the oak tree. "I'll have a better view from up here," she told me.

That didn't make the squirrels happy.

"Get out of our tree!" Zippy and Zappy shouted at the same time.

"Come on down and fight fair, Shadow," Scout yelped.

"You asked for it!" Shadow leaped down and landed on Scout's back.

"Scat, cat!" Scout shouted. He turned his head and tried to shoo Shadow off his back. But Shadow held on tight.

"Scat!" Scout yelled again. He reached his head back, opened his mouth, and took a big bite.

"Yooowwwww!" Scout yelped. "I bit my tail."

Shadow laughed. "Who's got the fur ball now?" she purred happily.

"Get off of him," Josie barked. She rushed over to help Scout.

Shadow leaped off Scout's back and out of the way, but Josie was going too fast to stop. She plowed into Scout and knocked him over.

Scout reached out his paws and the dogs started wrestling. I figured they were just playing. But that's not how the other animals saw it.

"Dog fight! Dog fight!" Zippy and Zappy cheered.

"This is more fun than TV," Shadow purred happily.

Zappy started cheering. "Scout, Scout, he's our man! If he can't beat her, no one can!"

"Josie, Josie, beat that Scout! Hit his head, hit his mouth!" Zippy cheered.

"That doesn't rhyme," Zappy told Zippy.

Zappy threw an acorn at Zippy. But he missed, and hit Shadow on the rear end.

"Rodents!" Shadow hissed angrily.

"Target practice!" Zippy and Zappy exclaimed. They started pelting acorns at Shadow, Scout, and Josie.

I'd had enough, so I headed back toward my house. Between the hissing cat, the barking dogs, the chattering squirrels, and the flying acorns, there was definitely trouble brewing out here. I was probably already in trouble with my mom for pushing Mia. I had a feeling that was enough trouble for one day.

Chapter 3

"How come you couldn't talk on the phone last night?" Leo asked me as we got off the bus and headed toward the school the next morning.

"Mia," I said simply.

I didn't have to give him any other explanation. Leo was my best friend. He knew what a tattletaling pain-in-the-neck my sister could be. It didn't really matter what I'd done.

"Did you bring your permission slip?" he asked.

"Definitely," I said as I opened the school door.

"Hey, what's going on here?" Leo asked as we walked into the school lobby. A huge crowd of kids had gathered around Principal Bumble's office.

"Out of the way. Move it." I heard Maxine's voice coming up behind me. "*Move!* Safety coming through."

She shoved Leo and me to the side and pushed her way to the front of the crowd.

When the kids moved aside for Maxine, I got to see what had happened.

Boy, what a mess!

Someone had toilet-papered Principal Bumble's office. There was paper everywhere — over the lights, around her chair, covering her desk, circling her lamp, dumped over her coat rack, and even wrapped around the giant rubber-band ball she keeps next to her computer. It was like it was Halloween, and this was the trick, not the treat.

"Who did this?" Principal Bumble asked. She didn't sound happy.

We all looked around to see if anyone was going to admit to the prank. But no one said anything.

"I'll get to the bottom of it," Maxine promised Principal Bumble. "After all, that's what school safeties do." She pointed to her bright-orange safety sash. Then she turned to the crowd of kids. "That's all, show's over," Maxine said. "Everyone get to class. There's nothing left to see."

Maxine was right. Looking at a toilet-papered office is only interesting for a minute. Besides, I didn't want to be late getting to my classroom. Mrs. Sloane really hates when kids are late. So Leo and I started down the hallway with the rest of the kids.

"Do you have a special baseball T-shirt for apple picking yet?" Leo asked me.

I knew what he meant. I have special T-shirts for everything. Like the one I was wearing today — my Tampa Bay Rays shirt. It brings me good luck on social studies quizzes. Last time I wore it I got a B plus.

"Not yet," I told Leo. "I'm thinking maybe my Westside Little League shirt would be good, though. That's the one I was wearing when I caught the game-winning ball last season."

"AAAAHHHH!"

Leo and I were about halfway down the hall when we suddenly heard a loud scream. It was coming from a room at the end of the hall.

I turned around and saw Nurse Kauffman standing in the doorway of the first-aid room. She was covered in white confetti.

We all started laughing. She looked like an abominable snow nurse.

Principal Bumble hurried over to the first-aid room. "What happened here?" she asked.

"Someone put a bucket of confetti up there." Nurse Kauffman spit a piece of white confetti out of her mouth and pointed to the top of her door frame. "When I opened the door, the bucket tipped over, and it all poured down on me." She looked down at the floor. "What a mess. I'll have to call Mr. Broomfield to clean up. He's not going to be happy."

I knew what Nurse Kauffman meant. Mr. Broomfield was the school janitor. He was a big grump on a good day. The extra work cleaning up the principal's office and now the first-aid room would make him even more miserable.

Principal Bumble headed back to her office. A moment later, we all heard her voice ring out over the PA system.

"It seems we have a prankster in our school today," Principal Bumble said. "I fully expect the person responsible for the pranks to stop immediately. We can't have someone running around playing tricks in school. If this continues, I will be forced to cancel the upper-school apple-picking trip. If I can't trust you to behave here at school, how can I trust you to behave at the apple orchard?"

Cancel the field trip? No way! Sure, the pranks had been kind of funny. But no one was laughing now.

Chapter 4

"Are you ready for the social studies quiz?" Elizabeth asked me as I sat down at my desk a few minutes later.

I pointed to my Tampa Bay Rays baseball shirt. "I've got all I need right here," I said.

Leo turned to the desk behind his. "How can you talk about social studies at a time like this?" he asked Elizabeth.

"A time like what?" she replied.

Leo looked at Elizabeth like she had three heads. "Didn't you hear what Principal Bumble said?" he asked her. "She's going to cancel the field trip if the person pulling the pranks doesn't stop."

"Oh that," Elizabeth said.

I couldn't help but laugh. That was such a Brainiac

thing to say. Only Elizabeth would be more focused on a quiz than the field trip.

"Yeah, *that*," Leo said. "Somebody has to figure out who's doing the pranking and make it stop."

"I thought Maxine was going to do that," I said.

"Maxine?" Leo made a face. "She can't even get kids to stop running in the halls. But you guys can solve a mystery. You've done it before."

Okay, that was weird. Leo hated when Elizabeth and I solved mysteries. He was always jealous.

"You *want* us to work on this mystery?" I asked him.

Leo nodded. "You two have experience," he said. "We need people who can solve a mystery working on this case."

Leo was right. Elizabeth and I had already solved some major mysteries. We'd found Leo's science fair plans after they'd been stolen. And we'd rescued my sister's tortoise, Tut, after he had been kidnapped. We were practically professional detectives.

Just then, Trevor sat down behind me. "I gotta agree with Cubby," he said. "You have got to stop this guy before he ruins everything."

Leo turned red when Trevor called him Cubby. He hates that nickname. His mom has been calling him Cubby since he was a baby because Leo is a lion name, and lion babies are called cubs. Trevor heard her say it one time and he started calling Leo "Cubby," too.

But Leo didn't argue with Trevor. For once, he and Trevor were agreeing on something. In fact, everyone in the class was on their side.

"You two have to do something," our classmate Sasha told us. "The whole school is depending on you. Well, not the whole school. Just the upper school. But there are a lot of kids in the upper school, and —"

"We get it," I said, interrupting Sasha. I wasn't trying to be rude, but sometimes you just have to stop Sasha in the middle of a sentence. Otherwise she'll keep talking forever.

"If everyone wants us to solve this mystery, that's what we'll have to do," Elizabeth said proudly.

"Great," Sasha said. "If you need any help, let me know."

I gulped. The last thing I needed was help from the other kids. Because if they found out that I talked to animals to get clues, they'd never let me live it down.

Elizabeth shot me a look. She's the only person who knows my secret. I haven't even told Leo because I'm afraid he'll think I'm really weird. I actually never told Elizabeth about it, either — she's just such a Brainiac she figured it out on her own.

"No, we can handle it," Elizabeth told Sasha. "Jack and I work as a team — a team of two."

"Well, your team better *win*," Trevor told her. "My cousin Bo is in fifth grade, and he's been on the apple-picking trip twice. All he ever talks about is how I haven't gotten to go yet. If this trip is canceled, I'm going to be *really* mad."

My palms got sweaty just looking at Trevor.

"Aachoooo!" Charlie sneezed suddenly.

"Gesundheit," I said.

"Thanks," Charlie mumbled. "I hate hay fever season."

"Get a tissue, will ya?" Trevor told him. "Your nose is running again."

"Sorry," Charlie said. He wiped his nose with his sleeve and then walked over to Mrs. Sloane's desk to get more tissues.

"How soon can you start?" Leo asked Elizabeth and me.

"As soon as we have free time," Elizabeth told him. "So probably right after the social studies quiz."

I hoped the quiz was short. The sooner we solved this mystery, the better. I really didn't want to miss my first upper-school field trip. And I definitely didn't want to be on Trevor's bad side, either.

Chapter 5

"Okay, Jack, let me get out my detective notebook," Elizabeth said. She and I were sitting on a bench in the playground during our class break. Mrs. Sloane always lets us run around in the schoolyard after a quiz. I guess she figures we need it.

Elizabeth had brought her backpack outside with her. That didn't surprise me, since Elizabeth brought her backpack everywhere. She probably even brought it with her to the bathroom, although I didn't know that for sure. She reached into it and handed me a plastic human skull, a bag of unpopped popcorn, and a tube of toothpaste. Finally, she pulled out the notebook.

I looked at the pile of junk. "What's all this stuff for?"

"If we get stuck somewhere for a long time, you'll be glad I have food," she said.

I frowned. Unpopped popcorn didn't sound too yummy.

"And toothpaste gives you fresh breath," Elizabeth added. "I hate bad breath."

"What about the skull?" I asked.

Elizabeth shrugged. "You never know when you'll need a good Halloween decoration." She picked up her pen and began to write.

THE MYSTERY OF THE PRACTICAL JOKER

"Okay, so what clues do we have so far?" Elizabeth asked me.

"Well, there's the toilet-papered principal's office, and the confetti over the nurse's door," I answered.

Elizabeth wrote all that down, and then studied the clues. "So we have to figure that the culprit was able to get into the school before school started," she said slowly. "And that he or she has access to lots of toilet paper."

Just then, Trevor came over to where we were sitting. "Tell me you've solved this mystery," he said.

I wished I could, but that was impossible. "We just got started," I said.

"I knew it," Trevor said. "You guys have nothing. Not even a suspect."

Now I was mad. *Really* mad. I don't know what came over me, but I picked up Elizabeth's plastic skull and shook it at Trevor!

"How's this for a suspect!" I shouted.

Trevor jumped and screamed really loud. Then he realized that the skull was fake. His face turned red.

"Not funny," Trevor told me. "Stop kidding around, and start solving mysteries." He stormed away.

Wow! I'd scared off Trevor the Terrible using nothing but a Halloween decoration! Amazing.

"See?" Elizabeth smiled. "You never know when something will come in handy."

Once again, the Brainiac was right. Now, if she and I could only find the right culprit, this would be the best day ever!

*   *   *

"Please take out your science homework," Mrs. Sloane said a few minutes later. We were back in the classroom and in our seats.

We all pulled out our worksheets on the parts of a flower. Well, all of us except Jada. She just sat there, staring at the board.

"Jada, where's your homework?" Mrs. Sloane asked.

"I ... um ... I forgot it." Jada pulled nervously on her short brown hair.

Mrs. Sloane nodded slowly. "We're going to be discussing the homework now. Since you don't have yours, you can go to the library and research how flowers get their water."

Jada picked up her notebook and a pen and walked out of the classroom. The rest of us watched as Mrs. Sloane drew a flower on the board and began asking us to name the different parts of the plant.

We had only named the roots and the stem when suddenly Jada came racing back.

"Finished already?" Mrs. Sloane asked her.

Jada shook her head. "Someone went into the library and took all the books off the shelves," Jada said. "They used them to build a huge pyramid."

"But that's impossible," Mrs. Sloane said. "The library was closed all morning while Mrs. Page was in a meeting. No one would have been allowed in there until now."

Jada shrugged. "Someone was definitely in there. And Mrs. Page is plenty mad. When I left she was going to find Mr. Broomfield to help her put the books back."

"Aachoo!" Charlie sneezed and reached into his desk for another tissue.

"Gesundheit," Mrs. Sloane said. She shook her head. "These pranks are getting to be a real problem."

"You have to talk to someone who was in the library at the same time as the prankster," Elizabeth whispered to me.

"You heard Mrs. Sloane," I whispered back. "No one was allowed in there all morning."

"Except the two goldfish in the bowl on Mrs. Page's desk," Elizabeth said. "They're always in the library."

"You want me to interview *fish*?" I asked her.

Elizabeth nodded. "It's no different than interrogating a dog, or a goat, or a horse, is it?"

She had a point. I had talked to all of those animals on our previous cases.

"Go now," Elizabeth said. "Before Mrs. Page finds Mr. Broomfield and brings him back there to help her with the books. If they're there, you can't interrogate the fish."

Interrogate was one of those detective words Elizabeth liked to use. It was just a fancy way of saying I had to ask the fish a bunch of questions.

"How am I going to get out of here?" I whispered.

"Do you have to go to the bathroom?" Elizabeth asked, wiggling her eyebrows. Why was she doing that?

"No," I said. "I went before I left the house this morning and —" I stopped as I realized what Elizabeth was saying. I didn't really have to go to the bathroom. I just had to use it as an excuse to get out of the classroom.

I raised my hand and asked Mrs. Sloane if I could use the hall pass. A minute later I was on my way to the library to talk to the goldfish. If anyone could explain what kind of fishy things had been happening in the library, they could!

Chapter 6

"We'll never get there at this rate."

"Get *where*? You never tell me where we we're going."

Uh-oh. As I opened the door to the library I heard two people arguing. That wasn't good. There was no way I could interview the fish if there were other people around.

I peeked my head in to see who was talking. But I didn't see anyone else in there. It was just me and the fish.

And that's when it hit me. It wasn't *people* who were arguing. It was the fish, Goldie and Fin.

"I think we passed that castle before," Goldie told Fin as she swam around the plastic castle that was stuck right in the middle of their fishbowl. "We're just going around in circles."

I had to get their attention. So I knocked on the bowl.

"Seaquake!" Goldie shouted. "Swim for cover!"

"Cover? Where?" Fin asked. "Those castle doors don't even open."

"It isn't a seaquake," I told the fish. "It's me. I wanted to get your attention."

"You couldn't come up with something better than a seaquake?" Fin asked me.

"Sorry," I apologized. "I was wondering if you guys could answer a few questions for me."

"We can try," Goldie said.

"Did you notice anybody in the library this morning?" I asked.

"You mean *out* of the water?" Fin asked.

I nodded. "Yeah. Someone with legs instead of fins," I told him.

"There was this one two-legged air breather," Goldie said. "That one started a major tsunami in the bowl."

"A tsunami?" I asked her.

"Yeah," she said. "Don't you know what that is?"

I figured it had to be some fish word I didn't know. I shook my head.

"It's a giant wave," Fin said. "It's usually caused by an underwater seaquake."

"Whoever the two-legged was, he hit the side of our bowl when he was moving some books," Goldie explained. "Water splashed right out."

I looked down at the desk. There wasn't a drop of water on it. "Are you sure?" I asked.

"Are you calling us liars?" Fin asked.

"No," I said. "I just was asking. Did you get a look at this two-legged person?"

"Nope," Fin said. "My eyesight's not so good."

"Mine, either," Goldie admitted. "I think it's a fish thing."

I frowned. Goldie and Fin hadn't given me a whole lot to go on. But I didn't have time to ask them any more questions. Mrs. Page and Mr. Broomfield would be back any minute. And Mrs. Sloane would probably be wondering why it was taking me so long to go to the bathroom.

I didn't want to have to explain that to anyone.

Elizabeth —

Whoever was in the library was in a bad mood and slammed into the fish bowl. Goldie and Fin said water splashed all over the place. But the desk was dry when I got there. That's all I could get out of the fish.

— Jack

I slipped the note into Elizabeth's hand while Mrs. Sloane was writing on the board. I expected Elizabeth to look disappointed after she read it. I hadn't gotten a whole lot of information out of Fin and Goldie.

But Elizabeth didn't look upset at all. In fact, she looked excited. I saw her pull out her detective notebook and scribble something down.

As we lined up to go to the art room, Elizabeth pulled me aside. "I think you may have just solved this case," she told me.

I looked at her. "How?"

"You said water was spilled, but by the time you got to the library it wasn't there anymore," Elizabeth told me.

"Yeah." I was completely confused. "So what?"

"So someone had to have cleaned up the mess," Elizabeth repeated.

"I repeat: so what?" I said.

Elizabeth took a deep breath. "Who cleans up the messes in this school?" she asked me.

That didn't take any thought at all. "Mr. Broomfield," I said. "He's been cleaning up messes all day long."

"Exactly," Elizabeth said. "Except he didn't clean up this mess completely. And he's going to be really sorry about that. He left us a big clue. One that's going to prove without a doubt that he's the school prankster!"

Chapter 7

"Tell me again why Mr. Broomfield would have pulled all the pranks," I asked Elizabeth as she and I snuck off in search of the janitor during our lunch period. "Why would he make more work for himself?"

"Cleaning up definitely makes Mr. Broomfield mad," Elizabeth agreed. "But I think that's because he never gets to do anything fun. We go on field trips, have carnivals, and go to parties. Have you ever seen Mr. Broomfield at a party?"

"Only at the end, when it's time to clean up the mess," I said.

"Exactly," Elizabeth said. "I think he's tired of being the only one in school who doesn't have fun. So he's making sure *no one* has any fun."

Once again, the Brainiac had a good point. And a lot of things did point to Mr. Broomfield. After all, he was the one who put toilet paper in the bathrooms, so he could have easily toilet-papered Principal Bumble's office.

But that didn't mean Elizabeth was right. We wouldn't know for sure until we talked to Mr. Broomfield.

I wasn't looking forward to that. Mr. Broomfield isn't the nicest guy in the world. He doesn't even like kids. Which is kind of weird, considering he works in a school.

"What are you doing here?" Mr. Broomfield asked grumpily as we entered the boiler room. "I'm on my break. You kids will just have to clean up your messes on your own."

I tried to walk away before we made Mr. Broomfield angrier. But Elizabeth grabbed my shirtsleeve and made me stay.

"There's something only *you* can straighten out for us," Elizabeth said. "What were you doing in the library this morning?"

"Helping Mrs. Page fix the bookshelves," Mr. Broomfield said. "The school prankster was at it again."

"No, I mean *before* that," Elizabeth said.

"I was cleaning up the toilet paper in Principal Bumble's office, and the confetti in the nurse's office," Mr. Broomfield told her. "Why do you need to know?"

"Because somebody cleaned up the water that spilled out of the fishbowl. And they did it before the library was open," I said, trying to sound as brave as Elizabeth.

Mr. Broomfield stared at me. "If it was already cleaned up, how do *you* know about it?" he asked.

Oops. "Um...I heard about it...um... somewhere," I said. I looked down at my feet. *Oh brother.* That hadn't sounded very detectivelike.

"If there was any water spilled, I didn't see it," Mr. Broomfield said. "The fish looked happy when I got there. They were swimming around in circles as always."

"So who cleaned up the water?" I asked.

"Who knows?" Mr. Broomfield said. "Maybe it cleaned itself up."

"Huh?" I asked.

"Actually, Jack —" Elizabeth said slowly.

I didn't like the sound of that. It seemed like Elizabeth wasn't so sure Mr. Broomfield was a suspect anymore. Which meant she had dragged me down to the boiler room for nothing.

"Hee hee hee!"

Suddenly, I heard a squeaky voice buzzing in my ear. I turned to see who it was, but Mr. Broomfield stopped me.

"Don't move, kid!" Mr. Broomfield shouted.

Uh-oh. What now?

Mr. Broomfield picked up a broom and swung. *Crack!* The broom hit the wall.

"Missed me!" the squeaky voice in my ear hummed.

"Darn wasps!" Mr. Broomfield grumbled. "They follow me wherever I go."

"Really?" I said aloud.

"It's a game we play," the wasp buzzed happily to me. "*Bug* the janitor. You should try it sometime."

I frowned. From the look on Mr. Broomfield's face, Elizabeth and I were *already* playing bug the janitor.

"I've been following him all morning — to the principal's office and the first-aid room," the wasp said. "I was really driving him crazy until the book lady came and got him because of a problem in the library. I don't like the library. It's too cold in there. So I flew down here to wait for him."

I thought about that. If Mr. Broomfield hadn't gone to the library until Mrs. Page got him, then he probably wasn't the one who spilled the fish's water.

Mr. Broomfield swung his broom again. *Clang!* This time he hit the metal boiler. "Darn wasps!"

45

"Let's get out of here," Elizabeth said as Mr. Broomfield lifted his broom again.

I followed her out of the boiler room. I didn't want to find out what Mr. Broomfield would do if the wasp landed on my shoulder!

"He's not the prankster," Elizabeth said as soon as we were out of the boiler room.

"I figured that out from what the wasp told me," I agreed. "But it still doesn't make sense. I don't believe that whole thing about the water cleaning itself up. Someone had to do it."

"Actually, water does dry up by itself," Elizabeth said. "It's called *evaporation*. If you leave water standing around long enough, it will turn into vapor that will mix with the air. It was probably just a few drops, so they evaporated quickly."

"I sure wish you'd thought of that *before* we interrogated Mr. Broomfield," I said.

"Why?" Elizabeth asked me. "Because he's so scary?"

"No," I answered. "Because it's lunchtime and I'm starving! Let's get to the cafeteria."

Chapter 8

"Where have you two been?"

We weren't in the cafeteria more than one minute when Elizabeth and I bumped into Maxine.

"We were trying to figure out who's been pranking everyone around the school," Elizabeth told her bravely.

Maxine gave her an odd look. "And did you?" she asked.

"Not yet," I told her. "We were close, but —"

"But you couldn't figure it out," Maxine said, cutting me off. "You third graders won't be able to solve this one." She smiled and pointed to her orange belt with her white-gloved hand. "That's why the school is lucky to have me."

"Why are you wearing gloves inside the cafeteria?" I asked her.

"These are safety gloves," Maxine said. "They give them to us for when it gets cold. I'm going outside to keep the playground safe during recess. It's pretty chilly out there today."

Weird. There were other safeties in the fifth grade. But Maxine was the only one wearing her gloves and her belt in the lunchroom.

"Come on, Jack," Elizabeth said. "Let's go eat."

"Okay," I agreed. "Today's my favorite meal. Breakfast for lunch. I hope there are still some pancakes left."

"Don't worry about the mystery anymore," Maxine said. "I've got everything under control."

I didn't get to find out about the pancakes because as soon as Maxine was gone, Leo and Trevor came rushing over.

"Tell me you found the prankster," Leo said.

"Wish I could," I told him. "But we haven't."

"Not yet," Elizabeth said. "We thought we had the right guy, but we were wrong. It happens all the time with mysteries."

"We don't have time for you to be wrong," Trevor told her.

Just then, a tall fifth grader named Bo walked over to us. He had straight hair and a whole lot of freckles. He also had a mean grin on his face.

"Don't feel too bad, Trev," Bo said. "So what if you and your friends don't get to go on the upper-school apple-picking trip? It's time the school did something new. Climbing trees, drinking cider, and eating fresh-baked apple pie is boring after you've done it twice. Of course, you'll never know, will you? Ha! See ya later, losers."

As Bo walked away, Trevor shook his head. "That guy is such a bully. I can't believe he's my cousin."

I didn't have any trouble believing that at all.

"You guys had better figure this mystery out fast!" Trevor said.

"We're doing our best," Elizabeth replied.

"Do better than your best," Trevor said. He stood up taller so he seemed even bigger than usual. Then he stomped off.

"This is really important, you guys," Leo said once Trevor was gone. "The whole school is counting on you two."

I was about to tell Leo that we were working as fast as we could. But before I could get a word out, a loud scream came from over by the salad bar. I turned in the direction of the scream and watched the lunch lady leap up on a chair. She was panicked about something.

"It sounds like the prankster has struck again!" Elizabeth grabbed me by the arm. "Come on!"

Elizabeth dragged me over to the salad bar to see what kind of monsterish thing could be there. Sure enough, there it was — sitting between the tomatoes and the lettuce — *Iggy, the little, green iguana from the science room.*

Iggy took a big bite out of a tomato. "Mmm . . . this tomato is pretty good," he hissed. "But I like the taste of red cabbage better. Hey! There's some!" He took a bite of an onion slice and then crawled over to the cabbage.

"Oh no! Don't let it eat the food!" The lunch lady reached down from the chair and tried to pull some of the vegetables out of the iguana's reach.

"Whooaaaa!" Suddenly, she lost her footing and let out a yell.

Splat! That was the sound of her landing face-first in the salad bar. I gasped, and Elizabeth's mouth dropped

open. Tomatoes, olives, cabbage, and croutons went flying all over the place.

That was all Bo needed to see. "Food fight!" he shouted as he lobbed a squishy tomato at his buddy, Chris.

"Incoming lettuce!" Chris shouted back. He threw a handful of lettuce leaves right at Bo, but somehow wound up hitting Maxine instead.

"I'm writing you both up," Maxine shouted at Bo and Chris.

"Heads up!" a fourth grader named Shelby yelled as she poured a handful of croutons over another girl's head.

A moment later, there were tomatoes, olives, and croutons flying all over the cafeteria. Teachers came running to stop the food fight.

Whoosh! I ducked as a handful of carrots flew past my head. Elizabeth wasn't as fast. She got pelted by a hailstorm of crunchy croutons.

"Hey!" Elizabeth shouted.

Maxine pulled out her safety notebook. "I'm writing *everybody* up!" she declared loudly.

For a second, I though about dumping the bowl of cucumber slices on Maxine's head. But I managed to stop myself.

Not Bo, though. He let Maxine know just what he thought of her writing people up. He grabbed a giant tomato from the salad bar, pulled his arm back like a major league pitcher, and . . .

Splat! That red, gooey tomato smacked Maxine right on her orange belt.

The lunch lady looked up from the salad bar. Her face was dripping with creamy Italian dressing. "Get that thing out of here!" she shouted, pointing to the iguana.

Any other time I would have laughed really hard at the sight of the lunch lady freaking out over a little iguana. But I knew Principal Bumble wasn't going to find the food fight funny at all. The field trip was canceled for sure.

Chapter 9

"Jack, you *have* to talk to that iguana," Elizabeth whispered to me as the teachers started instructing students to help clean up the mess.

Had Elizabeth gone crazy? "You want me to talk to the iguana *here*, in front of the whole school?" I asked her.

Elizabeth shook her head. "Of course not." She looked at the lunch lady. "Do you want us to take the iguana back to the science room?" she asked.

"Definitely," the lunch lady said. She wiped some salad dressing off the tip of her nose. "Please."

I scooped up the iguana. "You've had enough cabbage, Iggy," I whispered to him.

"Iggy." The iguana hissed and stuck his tongue out at me. "I've always hated that name. Couldn't you kids have come up with something more original?"

When we got to the science room I put Iggy back in his cage and gave him a handful of iguana food.

"Jack, hurry," Elizabeth said.

"Iggy, do you remember who took you out of your cage?" I asked him.

"I'm too stylish for a name like Iggy," he said. "I'd prefer to be called . . . Lancelot."

"Lancelot?" I asked.

Elizabeth started to write *Lancelot* in her notebook. Then she stopped. "There's no Lancelot at this school," she said.

"No. Iggy wants me to call *him* Lancelot," I explained.

"Call him anything he wants," Elizabeth said. "Just get the information."

"Okay, *Lancelot*," I said. "Do you remember who took you out of your cage?"

"I didn't get a good look," Iggy — er, Lancelot — admitted. "But the hands felt strange. Usually kids have sweaty, sticky hands, but these hands were dry and rough."

I frowned. That didn't tell me much.

"Did those onions give me bad breath?" Iggy asked as he hissed his iguana breath up toward me.

"You smell like an iguana," I said, trying to be nice. Then I put the lid back on his cage.

"What did he say?" Elizabeth asked me.

"He didn't get a look at the person's face," I said. "But whoever it was had dry, rough hands that felt different than most people's hands."

Elizabeth wrote that in her notebook and glanced up at the clock.

"Lunch is over. By now everyone is at recess," she said.

Oh man. That stunk. I was still starving. Being a detective definitely had some major drawbacks.

Elizabeth didn't seem to care about food at all, though. She was worried about something else. "We'd better get to the playground," she told me. "We don't want Maxine catching us wandering around the halls again."

It turned out we weren't the only ones wandering the halls. Just before we reached the door that led to the playground, we bumped into Charlie.

"What are you doing here?" Elizabeth asked him.

"I just came from the nurse's office," he explained. "I needed my allergy medicine. Falling leaves make me sneeze."

"I guess this is a bad time of year for you, huh?" Elizabeth asked him.

Charlie nodded. "There's a whole line of people at the nurse today. Lots of kids have allergies. Aachoo!"

I felt bad for Charlie. It couldn't be fun to be coughing and sneezing all the time.

"Did you guys figure out who the prankster is yet?" he asked me.

"Nope." I frowned.

But Charlie didn't frown.

"Whatever," he said. "It's not like I'm going to have any fun, anyway. I'll just be sneezing all the time."

"How come you're going on the field trip if you get all allergic outside?" I asked Charlie.

"My mom is making me," Charlie said. "She says I can't let my allergies keep me from being around the other kids. *Aaachooo!*"

I stepped back. Speaking for the other kids, I could safely say Charlie's mom was making a mistake. No kid wants to be around anyone who sneezes that much. I don't mind hanging out with Charlie when we're inside. But in an apple orchard, I'd rather stay away.

"Well, see you later," I said to Charlie.

"Have fun at recess," Charlie called as Elizabeth and I headed onto the playground.

"Heads up!"

A big red ball went flying past my head as Elizabeth and I stepped onto the playground. I ducked just in time.

"There's no dodgeball allowed in school!" Maxine shouted at the group of fifth graders who were throwing the ball.

"Who made you boss?" Bo asked her as he ran over and got his ball. Naturally, he was one of the kids playing dodgeball. Trevor and his cousin were the dodgeball kind of kids.

"This orange belt makes me boss," Maxine told him.

"So you're a safety," Bo said. "Big deal. Safeties are just tattletales with belts." He threw the ball at one of the kids standing near the wall. "Gotcha! You're out," he shouted, totally ignoring Maxine.

"I can't believe Maxine's worrying about dodgeball," I whispered to Elizabeth. "She should be helping us with this mystery."

"We don't need help!" Elizabeth said angrily. "I solve mysteries all the time. I can figure out who did it by the third chapter."

"That's a mystery in a book," I reminded her. "This is real life."

"We just have to try harder," Elizabeth insisted.

I wasn't sure I *could* try harder. I'd already interviewed two fighting fish, a janitor with an attitude, and an iguana with bad breath.

That seemed like plenty of hard work to me.

Chapter 10

"You guys had better stick to being kissy faces," Trevor said to Elizabeth and me as our class started walking toward the busses at the end of the school day. "Because you stink at being detectives."

"We are *not* kissy faces!" I shouted back at him. Which was the truth. I didn't say that we didn't stink as detectives. Because frankly, we did. At least that's how I felt. It had never taken Elizabeth and me more than a few hours to solve a mystery before. But here the whole school day was over, and we hadn't solved anything.

"Hey, did you third graders hear?" Bo asked, as he and two of his friends walked over to us. "Looks like you can make plans for playdates on Friday afternoon. Principal Bumble was really mad about that food fight. And they had to clean out the whole salad bar because that iguana touched everything. Mr. Broomfield really freaked out when he saw all that food all over the place, too."

"Did Principal Bumble cancel the field trip?" Elizabeth asked him.

"Not yet, but you can bet she will," Bo said. He looked at his cousin. "Don't worry, Trev. Maybe you'll get to go apple picking before you graduate from *high school*." He started laughing.

Trevor glared at his cousin. And then he glared at Elizabeth and me. "I don't know why we thought you two kissy faces could solve anything."

I looked over at Leo. My best pal. I was hoping he'd say something to defend me. But Leo didn't say a word. He was as mad at us as everyone else.

Just then, Maxine came over to us. "Okay, everybody onto the busses," she said. "Move it."

"Did you find out anything else about the prankster?" Elizabeth asked.

"That's for me to know, and you to find out," Maxine said. "Which you never will because you're not a safety. You can't do anything to stop these practical jokes."

I was beginning to think maybe Maxine was right. Elizabeth and I had no suspects and no clues. And for some reason that made Maxine very happy.

"Move it," she said. "Move it. Move it."

"Move it. Move it. Move it."

The next day at school started just the way the previous one had ended. Maxine was standing at the door yelling at everyone. But this time she was sending us into the school instead of rushing us out of it.

"You think Maxine sleeps here?" I asked Elizabeth. "No matter what time it is or where I've been, she's already here."

"As a safety she has to be around when everyone's coming and going," Elizabeth said. "She has to get here early and leave late."

"I don't know why she bothers," I said. "No one around here ever listens to her, anyway. They never listen to anyone on the safety patrol."

I looked over at Maxine. She was writing something in her safety notebook. I could see her white-gloved fingers moving really, really fast. I couldn't write with gloves on if I tried. But I figured Maxine had a lot of practice at it.

"Come on, Jack," Elizabeth urged. "We're supposed to go right to the science room this morning to check on our bean plants, remember? It's on the other side of the school."

"Okay," I said, trailing behind her. I didn't like spending so much time with Elizabeth. It was more fun hanging out with Leo before school. He wasn't obsessed with things like checking on how much his bean plant had grown in the past week. But since no one — not even Leo — seemed to be talking to me anymore, Elizabeth was the only friend I had left.

Naturally, Elizabeth and I were the first ones waiting at the door of the science room that morning. But eventually the other kids showed up. By the time Mrs. Sloane showed up at the lab, we were all there.

"Now, I want you to be sure to count the number of leaves on your plants and measure the stems so you can compare them with last week's growth," Mrs. Sloane said as she opened the door to the science lab. "And then we . . . OH MY GOODNESS!"

OH MY GOODNESS!

Mrs. Sloane's face turned bright red. Then it turned pale white. For a minute I thought she was going to pass out — or worse.

Something awful was obviously going on inside the science lab. *But what was it?*

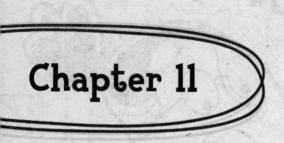

Chapter 11

Elizabeth and I pushed past Mrs. Sloane to get into the science lab. What we saw was kind of wild and amazing.

I gasped. "How did that happen?" I asked Elizabeth.

Elizabeth shook her head. "I've never seen anything like it before," she replied.

We were staring at the animal cages over by the windows. There was Iggy, a hamster named Harry, and Rosa, the guinea pig.

It was Rosa who had caught everyone's attention. She was usually brown and white. But today, Rosa the guinea pig was *bright green*!

Now I knew why Mrs. Sloane was so upset. Rosa looked really weird.

"Whoa!" Trevor shouted out. "Check out Rosa." He ran over to her cage.

"Trevor, stay away from the guinea pig," Mrs. Sloane said. "She could be sick."

Elizabeth shook her head. "I don't think there's any illness that would turn a guinea pig's fur green," she said.

"Well, *something* happened to her," Mrs. Sloane told us.

"I think it's another prank," Elizabeth said.

"It's a mean one," Sasha said. "Who would paint a guinea pig?"

"I don't think it's paint," I told Sasha. "I know that color green. It's powdered fruit drink. Limeade. That's my favorite flavor."

Elizabeth walked over to Rosa's cage. There was some green powdery stuff around the edges of the cage. My partner dipped her finger into it and then sniffed. "You're right," she said. "It's limeade. But it's really sticky, as if someone only used a little bit of water."

"Is that dangerous for Rosa?" Sasha asked.

Elizabeth shook her head. "I don't think so," she assured her. "It's just sugar, water, and food coloring."

"Aachoo!" Charlie sneezed. "I've gotta get out of here. Hamster and guinea pig fur make me sneeze."

"We're all getting out of here," Mrs. Sloane said. She shook her head. "This practical joke is going to be the last straw, I'm afraid."

Everyone in the class turned to stare at Elizabeth and me. What did they want us to do? It wasn't like we weren't working on the case! I'd have liked to see any of them try to solve it.

"You've gotta talk to Rosa, and fast," Elizabeth whispered to me as our class walked out of the science lab.

"Tell me something I don't know," I whispered back. "I'm going back there right now."

"But Mrs. Sloane isn't going to let —"

I didn't wait for Elizabeth to finish her sentence. "I forgot my notebook in the lab," I shouted out suddenly.

Mrs. Sloane looked at me. "I didn't see you take a notebook from your backpack, Jack," she said.

"You . . . uh . . . you must have been too busy looking at Rosa to see," I said. "But I did. And I have to get it."

"Okay," my teacher sighed. "Go get it. And then hurry back to class."

I turned and ran back into the room, letting the door slam shut behind me.

71

"Will you stop slamming the door?" Harry the hamster squealed angrily. "What is it with you kids? That's the third time this morning someone has woken me up."

"Is it anyone's fault you sleep all day?" Iggy said.

"The first time I had just fallen asleep," Harry told him. "There's nothing more annoying than being woken up when you've just fallen asleep."

"That's true," I agreed. "Are you telling me someone came in here before my class did?"

"Oh yeah," Harry said.

"The kid wanted to play with me," Rosa said. "How do you think I turned this color?"

"Do you know who turned you green?" I asked her.

Rosa shook her head. "Whoever it was sneezed a few times. And the kid wasn't very nice."

"Why do you say that?" I asked.

"Usually after a kid plays with me, I get a chew stick," Rosa said. "But not this time."

"Thanks for the info," I said. I grabbed a chew stick and put it in her cage.

"Hey, tell me the truth," Rosa said. "Do you think I look better with green fur?"

"You look great," I assured her. What was I supposed to say? You look like a furry lime Popsicle?

"Thanks." Rosa grabbed her chewstick. Then she turned around and showed me her green guinea pig rear end.

I figured that meant this conversation was over.

Chapter 12

"So?" Elizabeth asked, as I sat down on the floor beside her. Mrs. Sloane had given our class some quiet reading time. Elizabeth was in the back of the room all by herself, reading a new mystery book.

"I didn't get much," I whispered. "Just that the person who covered Rosa in green limeade woke up Harry the hamster just as he'd fallen asleep."

Elizabeth thought about that for a minute. "Then it must have happened pretty early this morning," she said.

"How do you know?" I asked her.

"Because hamsters are nocturnal," she said.

"Nock what?" I asked. I really hate when Elizabeth talks like a Brainiac.

"Nocturnal," Elizabeth repeated. "It means they sleep in the daytime. So the prankster must have come into the science room early this morning, just as the sun came up and Harry was falling asleep."

"Oh," I said. That was interesting, I guess. But it didn't tell us much.

"Anything else?" Elizabeth asked me.

"The person who put the limeade on Rosa sneezed," I said.

"Now, *that's* important!" Elizabeth said. She wrote "sneezed" in her detective notebook.

"Why?" I asked her.

"Charlie sneezes a lot," she pointed out. "And he said their fur makes him sneeze even more."

"Yeah. But if guinea pigs make him sneeze, why would he pull a prank that used a guinea pig?" I smiled proudly. I loved it when I outsmarted Elizabeth.

"Charlie doesn't want to go on a field trip to an apple orchard," Elizabeth said. "There are too many trees there. Maybe he figured it was worth a few extra sneezes to stop the trip."

Hmm . . . I hadn't thought of it that way.

Elizabeth got up and walked over to where Charlie was sneezing and reading. I followed close behind.

"We need to talk to you," Elizabeth told Charlie.

"*Aachoo*," Charlie sneezed.

"Gesundheit," Elizabeth said. "Where were you this morning before school started? I didn't see you in the playground when I got here."

"I went right to the nurse's office. I had to give her my new medicine." He stopped for a minute, and looked at us. "Wait a minute. You two don't think I painted Rosa, do you?"

"Well, you don't want to go on the field trip," I said. "And you sneeze a lot."

"What does sneezing have to do with anything?" Charlie asked me.

Oops. I couldn't tell Charlie how I knew the prankster sneezed while he was dying Rosa's fur. That would be giving away my superpower.

"Forget the sneezing," Elizabeth said. "You were in the building before any other kid. You had a chance to dye Rosa's fur."

"I break into hives when I touch a guinea pig," Charlie said. "Do you see any hives on my arms?" He rolled up his sleeves. There weren't any red bumps.

Elizabeth looked at her hands for a moment. Then she looked at Charlie's. Finally, she frowned. "I'm sorry, Charlie," she said. "We should have known it wasn't you."

"Yeah, you should have known bet — *aachooo*!" Charlie sneezed.

"Gesundheit," I said.

As I started to follow Elizabeth back to the other side of the room, I asked her, "*Why* should we have known it wasn't him?"

77

Elizabeth held up her hand. There was still green limeade on her fingers. "It takes a long time to wash this stuff off," she said.

Now I got it. "So all we have to do is find someone with green fingers and we have the prankster," I said.

Elizabeth nodded. "And we'd better hurry," she told me. "If we give the prankster enough time to really scrub, eventually the powder will come off."

"And our whole case will go down the drain," I added.

Chapter 13

"Hey, Elizabeth, slow down," I shouted as my partner hurried through the halls.

"We have to hurry, Jack," Elizabeth said. "I want to be standing at the door of the cafeteria when kids come in so I can check their hands for traces of limeade powder."

I wasn't exactly sure how Elizabeth planned on doing that. What was she going to do — stand there by the door demanding to inspect everyone's hands? That's the kind of thing a mom does, not a third grader.

Elizabeth turned around to see where I was heading and *BAM!* She bumped right into Trevor's cousin Bo. His notebook fell out of his hands and onto the floor.

"Watch where you're going!" Bo exclaimed.

"I'm sorry —" she began to apologize. Then she stopped herself and looked at the floor. There was a packet of limeade powder next to Bo's notebook.

"Whoa!" I exclaimed. "You're the prankster!"

Bo gave me a weird look. "What are you talking about?"

"He's talking about that," Elizabeth said. She pointed to the packet of green powder.

"Where did that come from?" Bo asked me.

"Shouldn't we be asking *you* that?" I replied.

Just then, Maxine came around the corner. "What are you two doing in the halls during lunch period again?" she asked Elizabeth and me.

"Catching the prankster," I told her. I pointed to the packet of powder on the floor.

Maxine started to smile. She pulled out her safety notebook. "I'm going to report you, Bo. You're going to be in major trouble." She smiled. "I might even get a medal for this."

"But I didn't do anything," Bo said. He actually sounded scared.

"We caught you red-handed," I told him.

Elizabeth shook her head. "You mean green-handed," she said. "And I don't think we did. The only thing Bo has on his hands is dirt."

"So what?" Maxine said.

"So the evidence would be green," Elizabeth told her. "That's the color drink powder the prankster used to paint the guinea pig."

Maxine looked at the packet of drink powder. "Limeade," she said. "That's green."

Elizabeth gave Maxine a funny look. "What are you doing here, anyway?" she asked. "Were you following Bo? Or us?"

"I'm a safety," Maxine said. "I can go anywhere, any time. I'm just doing my job."

"Does your job include turning guinea pigs green?" Elizabeth asked.

"Of course not." Maxine bit her lip and looked away.

"Why weren't you surprised that someone had turned Rosa green?" Elizabeth asked her. "You weren't in the science room when we found her that way."

Maxine bit her lip a little harder. Then she said, "I don't have to answer your questions. You aren't a safety."

But she didn't sound as tough as she had before. She sounded a little scared.

Suddenly, it all started to make sense. "You can go anywhere," I said. "No one would question you. It's what safeties do."

"Exactly," Maxine said. "And safeties don't dye guinea pigs."

"Really?" Elizabeth asked. "Well if you didn't do it, then you can take off your gloves and show us your hands."

"Why would I to do that?" Maxine snickered. "I'm going out to the playground in a minute, and my hands will get cold."

"But we're inside now," I pointed out.

"And it would prove you're innocent," Elizabeth said.

"I don't have to prove anything," Maxine said. "I'm a safety." Suddenly she didn't sound so sure of herself. She turned and started to walk away.

But Elizabeth grabbed her by the arm and stopped her. Then she yanked the glove right off Maxine's hand.

"Hey!" Maxine reached for the glove. And when she did, she flashed her bright green limeade-colored fingers at us.

"You *are* the prankster!" I shouted excitedly.

Elizabeth smiled proudly. "Maxine gets to school before everyone," she said. "It gives her plenty of time to pull pranks. And those gloves were a big clue. They cover her stained fingers."

And gloves are rough and dry. Just like Iggy said, I thought.

"No wonder you didn't want us investigating," Elizabeth said. "You were afraid we'd solve the case."

"Which we did," I added proudly.

"You two little jerks have ruined everything," Maxine said. "*I* was supposed to be the one who stopped the

84

prankster. Bo was supposed to get in trouble. That's why I put the packet of limeade in his notebook during math class."

"You were framing me?" Bo asked.

"It was time someone got you in trouble," Maxine told Bo. "You think you don't have to follow the rules. You think you don't have to listen to me, but everyone has to listen to the safeties. I figured if I could stop the prankster and save the field trip —"

"Then people would think safeties were important," Elizabeth finished Maxine's thought.

"Exactly," Maxine said.

"But why frame Bo?" I asked her.

"Yeah, why frame me?" Bo repeated. "What did I do?"

"How about run in the halls, play dodgeball, and start a food fight in the cafeteria?" Maxine told him. "I have a whole list of rules you've broken. This would have been payback for everything."

Elizabeth shook her head. "You have to turn yourself in," she told Maxine.

"No I don't," Maxine said. "Who's going to tell on me? You? Principal Bumble would never believe the two of you over a safety." She turned to Bo. "And she won't believe you, either. You're such a troublemaker."

"But we've got proof," Elizabeth said. "And it's right there on your fingers."

Maxine frowned. But she didn't argue. How could she? She knew we'd caught her — green-handed!

Chapter 14

"I'm glad you guys solved the mystery," Leo said as our class rode around the apple orchard in a horse-drawn wagon. We had just spent about an hour picking and eating apples. "Thanks."

"You're welcome," I told him. I was having a really great time on the field trip. Everyone was treating Elizabeth and me like we were heroes.

"I have to hand it to you two kissy faces," Trevor said.

"We are *not* kissy faces," I told him for the gazillionth time. "We're detectives."

"And good ones," Elizabeth added.

"I still can't understand why Maxine would want to stop the field trip," Leo said.

"She didn't," Elizabeth explained. "She just wanted everyone to think she was important."

"Well, now she's *absent*," Trevor said.

He was right. Maxine hadn't been allowed to go on the apple-picking trip. And she didn't get to be a safety anymore, either. I wondered which part she felt worse about.

"Aachoo!" Charlie let out a huge sneeze. "I am so allergic to horses."

"Aachoo!" Just then, the horse pulling our cart let out a massive sneeze. "I am so allergic to kids!" he whinnied.

I laughed.

"What's so funny?" Leo asked.

I didn't answer. Instead, I took a big bite out of a yellow delicious apple and grinned.

My partner and I had done a great job this time. And everyone was happy about it.

"Aachoo!"

"Aachoo!"

Except for Charlie and the horse, anyway.

Calling All Detectives!
Be sure to read all the
Jack Gets a Clue mysteries!

Here's a sneak peek of
The Case of the Loose-Toothed Shark . . .

"Let's go look at the huge shark tooth," Alyssa said. "The tooth —" She stopped and stared at the shelf. "The tooth is gone!" she exclaimed. "It's been stolen!"

Frank the guard came running over. "Oh no," he said. "It must have happened while I walked into the other room."

"Did you see anyone in here before it disappeared?" Alyssa asked.

"Yeah, a couple of kids. One of them was really interested in it." He looked around and then pointed. "There he is."

"Me?" I asked nervously. "I didn't steal anything."

My dad looked at me. "If you say you didn't take it, you didn't take it," he said. But he didn't sound one hundred percent sure.

"We have to go help with the little kids," my mother told Elizabeth and me. "We can talk about this later."

As my parents walked off, I sat down on a bench near the giant freshwater fish tank on the wall. Elizabeth sat down next to me.

"I know you didn't steal anything," she said.

Just then I heard kissing noises.

"Kiss. Kiss. Smooch! I love you," someone said.

Oh great. That was all I needed.

"We are *not* kissy faces!" I shouted.

Elizabeth laughed and pointed to two white fish near the front of the tank. They looked like they were kissing. "Those are guorami fish," she said. "They're also called *kissing fish*."

Talk about embarrassing. The fish had been speaking to each other. But I was the only person who had heard them.

I turned to Elizabeth. "Forget about the fish. It looks like we have a new mystery on our hands," I said. "We have to find out who stole that tooth — and fast!"